the tale of
TILUNA

Josiah de Bono

ISBN: 9798302094728

The Tale of Tiluna © 2024 Josiah de Bono

All rights reserved.

For inquiries, please email **WanderingHedgehogPublishing@gmail.com**

No part of this book may be replicated, reproduced, or reused without permission from the author.

This is a work of fiction, all likenesses to characters real or otherwise are purely coincidental.

For all those I have ever, and will ever call friend.

I miss you all.

1

Once, when I was a grown-up, I had an imaginary friend. My friend wasn't really imaginary mind you, but that's what grown-ups would like to hear.

If I didn't say this, a grown-up might mistake this book for one of very serious matters. They'll open it up and read a few pages, and then they'll get very confused when something doesn't seem serious at all.

"What utter nonsense!" they'll say as they snap the book shut. Then they'll go and read something much more useful and worthwhile. So, for their sake, my friend was imaginary.

You must forgive them for this, they haven't felt curiosity in a long time. But we can't quite blame them for that, being a grown-up certainly isn't easy.

The thing about us grown-ups is that because we stop asking silly questions, we no longer find the answer to a lot of things. We just don't think some things are that important.

Children on the other hand are good at asking questions. They see a world full of question marks whilst we grown-ups only see full stops.

It is a cruel injustice that when we age, we lose our curiosity. We grown-ups eagerly exchange it for judgment, thinking that judgment makes us wise.

But what wisdom is there without curiosity in the first place? Wisdom isn't how old someone happens to be. Wisdom is how curious they have been. Some people learn more in a year than others do in twenty.

So, dear reader, if you take anything from me, if you take anything from the story of my imaginary friend, please just remember to stay curious when you grow up.

Because if you dare to be curious, you will be pleasantly surprised. If you dare to be curious, you will never grow old. If you dare to be curious, you will be nothing but kind.

2

Tiluna lived alone, in a lighthouse lost at sea. And every night, under that silver sky of stars, she would sit atop her lighthouse home and search the far blue sea.

But of what she was searching for she never really knew, except that it was very important that she should keep looking.

"Look out for lost things," she was told, "that's what a lighthouse keeper would do."

And so there she stayed, night after night, dawn after dawn, peering into the infinite waves, looking for anything lost. Nights turned to winters, and winters turned to years, until the seasons became nothing more than different types of stars.

But of lost things Tiluna found none. No boats, no ships, no sailors marooned at sea.

She had never found a single thing.

Until one night, when the moon was so bright that it shone like a phantom sun, and the stars danced upon the waves in their thousands,

one night, she found me.

3

I was completely and utterly lost. Clinging to little wooden planks, adrift and far out to sea. My boat had all but broken, for the sail was torn, and the hull nearly snapped in two. A terrible storm had battered it so badly that it could barely stay afloat.

There I was, lying on my makeshift raft, waiting for it to slowly sink below the waves. I remember going to sleep that night thinking I would never be found, for I had not seen another person in a *very* long time.

So when morning came, a little girl with silver hair was the last thing I expected to see.

"Are you lost?" she said.

"What?"

"Are you lost?" she repeated. "Because I'm supposed to look out for lost things."

I got to my feet, but my boat was gone. I could no longer feel the waves gently rocking beneath me.

"Where am I?" I asked her.

"Well then you must be lost," she concluded, crossing her arms in satisfaction, "for found people don't ask where they are."

I thought I must have been dreaming, or very dehydrated, possibly both. But dream or not, there we were, standing on the rocks of a lonely little lighthouse. A lighthouse? What was a lighthouse doing here so far out to sea?

You will know that lighthouses are often found on the coast, to help lost ships find the harbour. They certainly had no use this far out. I made a point of asking her this.

"Lighthouses are for finding lost things," she chanted back. "And if it were on the coast, I wouldn't have found you."

"You found me?" I asked. "Where is my boat? Did it sink?"

She seemed very confused at this.

"What's a boat?" she said.

"What's a boat?" I was astonished. "You live in a lighthouse, and you don't know what a boat is?"

But she ignored my question altogether, and repeated hers yet again, "What's a boat?"

"It's how people float," I said. "It's how people float, and it's made of wood."

I didn't really have time for this, I needed to get back home immediately. People would be starting to worry about me.

"Is that a boat?" she said, pointing to something on the rocks. And there it lay, the washed-up wreckage of my ship.

I felt a great lump of disappointment at the sight of my broken boat. How on Earth could I sail back home in that? It wasn't even in one piece!

"So how does it float?" she said.

But I didn't answer. I hobbled over to it with all the strength left in my knobbly legs. It was a mess. Barely the boat it was when I set out from England. Nothing but scattered pieces of soggy wood and broken rope were left of the poor thing.

But I had little time to waste. I got to work

immediately, picking up pieces in one hand and stacking them in the other.

"How does it float?" the little girl repeated, her head still tilted to one side. But I didn't have time to answer, it was very important that I returned home immediately.

After ignoring her questions for a good minute, it wasn't long before the little girl started to copy what I was doing, gathering bits of wood and stacking them on top of each other, one by one.

"What do we do with these?" she asked. "Are we making castles? Or do we keep stacking them up to see how high they go?"

"*We*, don't do anything," I said rather rudely, "*I*, am going to repair my boat and get back home."

But even if I managed to fix it, and even with all the confidence in the world, I still didn't know in which direction home was. I didn't even know where here was! So I asked her.

"How did you get here?"

"What do you mean?" she said.

"I mean, how did you arrive here?" I was beginning to get very annoyed at her ignorance. It would have been much simpler to sort things out with a fellow grown-up. So I asked her where I might find one.

"Do your parents own this lighthouse?"

But she seemed confused at this.

"Your parents are inside, aren't they?"

"What are parents?" she said.

"Grown-ups, you know, your grown-ups."

But these words seemed as unfamiliar to her as all the last.

"Are you a grown-up?" she asked me.

"Well yes, just about."

"What makes you a grown-up?"

Her curiosity was beginning to get on my nerves.

"I've lived long enough to stop asking silly questions," I snapped back. "And I've grown to my fullest height."

But this did not satisfy her.

"How can a question be silly?" she wondered.

"Because silly questions have obvious answers," I moaned impatiently. "And it would be silly to not know something obvious. Now please, leave me alone."

I returned to stacking the little pieces of

wood, feeling a great sense of victory in silencing her.

But my victory was somewhat short-lived, when she asked,

"If you do not know what something is, and have the chance to find out, wouldn't it be silly to continue not knowing?"

I must admit she was a very *odd* little girl, not to know grown-ups, or to live in a lighthouse and to have never seen a boat before.

As she said this, a plank of wood slipped in my hand, and a great big splinter lodged itself in my finger. Between the sudden pain of the splinter, and the slow frustration of constant questions, I got angry and shouted something rather horrid,

"Well one day you'll become a grown-up and you'll understand!"

For a while there was a silence between us, perhaps I shouldn't have said that.

"No, no I'm quite alright thank you," she said. "Being incuriously grown-up sounds rather silly."

"Well where I come from," I mumbled, "we don't have much say in the matter."

She paused for a moment, contemplating the oddness of it all,

"And where is it that you come from?"

"England," I replied, still nursing the little splinter wound on my finger. She must have heard of England, everyone who knows anything would have heard of England. But the shrug of her shoulders told me she had not. Before she could ask me a billion questions until the end of time, I had the brilliant idea of asking her one.

"Have you always been on your own out here?"

"Yes."

"Don't you get lonely?"

Then she looked at me with that curious stare yet again,

"What's lonely?" she said.

I explained it to her.

"Do stars get lonely? Or is it just people?"

But of course, I pretended not to hear such a ridiculous question, and returned to picking up the scattered driftwood.

She repeated her question once again. She wasn't one to let a question go unanswered.

"Do stars get lonely? Or is it just people?"

"Of course stars don't get lonely!" I moaned, as if the answer was obvious. "Don't be so ridiculous."

"Why is it ridiculous?" she said. "I'd be lonely if I were all alone up there."

I huffed a great impatient sigh. Was this little girl going to ask me every question she didn't know the answer to? Why couldn't she be like the good little children back home in England. The ones who knew that questions should only be asked in school.

"Stars don't get lonely," I said. And that was that.

"Why?"

"Because they don't."

"Why?"

"They just don't."

"Why?"

"Because they don't have feelings."

I could almost hear the words 'why' begin to form in her mind, so I quickly said,

"Look. I'm very busy here. I need to rebuild my boat. And it would be built a lot faster if I didn't have to answer all your silly questions."

I didn't mean to be rude, and I definitely didn't mean to hurt her feelings, but I was very stressed and very tired. I'm sure you've met a great many grown-ups like this.

You must forgive us for this, we grown-ups can be awfully grumpy people when we're tired.

"Well, I'm going to bed," she said, bringing an end to our conversation. "I hope you build your boat in time."

"To bed?" I replied. "It's the middle of the morning?"

"Exactly. The daytime is for sleeping. Goodbye."

I suppose it was now my turn to not know something obvious. So without further ado, she trundled up the lighthouse steps, and disappeared behind the little blue door.

And that was how I met Tiluna.

4

What an odd little girl, I thought to myself. How had she lived here all alone? And for how long I wonder? What peculiar circumstances had brought her here? And stranger still, who had built this lighthouse? This lonely lamp lost at sea that was of no use to anyone.

But I didn't have long to ponder these mysteries. Time was ticking on and on, and I needed to make good use of it.

So I continued to collect the broken bits and pieces all morning, until I had them neatly stacked on the rocks beside the lighthouse wall. Hundreds of little planks just sitting there, one on top of the other.

My boat would take a great many days of work to repair, and even then, there were still a great many pieces missing. That night I wanted to keep working, but I was so exhausted. And a tired mind is of no use to anyone.

So after that long day, I sat atop the lighthouse platform, and watched the sun say its farewells.

If you ever have the chance to see the sun

slowly set into the sea, I must advise you to do so. In all my long years, I have never come across a person, child or grown-up, who regretted watching the sunset.

I was starting to worry that I wouldn't get back home, that like Tiluna, I wouldn't leave this lonely lighthouse lost at sea. Perhaps this was how she found herself here. Perhaps this is why she'd never heard of grown-ups, or England or anything a child back home should know of.

My boat was damaged very badly, and it would take days to patch it up. But even if I did, what then? Without my maps and compass, I wouldn't even be able to point myself in the right direction, let alone sail there.

How terribly lost I felt that night, and how terribly sad my family would be if I didn't make it home. I couldn't bear the thought of never going home. And so, for the first time in a great many years, I cried and cried.

"Good night!" came Tiluna's sleepy voice from behind.

She had finally woken up.

It was a good night. A beautiful night. The

silver stars above us reflected in the calm ocean waves below, dancing in their thousands, lighting the very sea itself with silver fire.

"Why are you crying?" she asked.

I wiped away my tears as quickly as I could, and forced a comforting smile that didn't quite reach my eyes.

Crying isn't something grown-ups like to do in public. We grown-ups like to pretend that all is well, but then we quickly shed a hundred tears when we think no one is watching. Grown-ups save their tears for themselves, and no one really knows why.

"Don't be sad about your boat," she said sitting down beside me. "We'll build you a new one, a better one!"

But it wasn't the boat that I was sad about, it was the thought of never going home. Oh how I wished to get back home.

"Look!" she whispered, pointing to the sky. A flurry of shooting stars flew past in their hundreds, burning and blazing across the night, before vanishing into the ever-growing dark.

"I've always wondered what they are," she

whispered in awe.

"Meteorites," I said.

"What are meteorites?"

I suppose I knew that was coming. But I wasn't angry anymore. I think all my anger before was just misplaced sadness. I felt quite guilty that I'd been so rude to her earlier, so I did my best to make amends.

"Meteorites," I said. "Little bits of rock that burn when they fall from the sky. It's not often you see those around."

"Really?!" she gasped. "I see them every night from here."

She turned her head as a second group passed.

"I always thought they were falling stars. That if a star gets too sad, it falls from the sky. That's why I wanted to know if stars get lonely."

Her smile faded as she said this. "Do you get falling stars in England?"

Whenever I answered one of Tiluna's questions, she always had another at the ready. As if your response had set off a never-ending domino chain of questions and answers. Her curiosity seemed to have no end, not until she knew absolutely everything about anything.

I suppose we'd all be curious about a world we've never heard of before. For all she knew were the waves below and the stars above.

"We probably do," I replied, still looking to the sky.

"Why? Don't you know?"

"I don't do much star gazing back home."

"Oh," she said, as if that answered it. "Why?"

"I don't have the time. I'm busy in the evenings."

"What's time?"

What's time? To think this little girl had lived this long without knowing what *time* was.

"Time!" I said, pointing to my battered old wristwatch. "How we measure the day, how we know where to be, and more importantly, when to be there!"

"And your time device tells you all that?"

"No no," I sighed. "We keep time for the benefit of others. So everything happens at the proper time, so everyone knows when something should be done. And most importantly, so we know how much time we have left to do something."

Tiluna thought about this for a moment, and then giggled uncontrollably.

"That sounds silly," she decided. "If I had time, I wouldn't waste it worrying how much I had left."

She had the most amazing laugh.

"It's not that simple," I said. "We can't just do whatever we want when we want to."

But she didn't reply. She was too busy watching the falling stars.

We sat in silence for a while, our feet dangling over the platform's edge.

Understandably, children do not understand grown-ups. How could they? For they have not become one yet. To a child, grown-ups are illogical and mindbogglingly bizarre. So many rules to follow, so many hoops to jump through, and not even half of them seem like a good idea.

They simply cannot comprehend what it means to be grown-up.

But this is not strange. You wouldn't expect an acorn to know what it's like to be an oak tree.

But what is peculiar, what is very bizarre, is

that most grown-ups do not understand children. How can this be possible? How can someone forget something so important?

I was entirely guilty of this, as I'm sure most grown-ups like me often are. But now I suppose looking back at it, becoming a grown-up simply means forgetting what it is to be a child.

"Look!" she said once more, pointing to the sky. "See that! That silver one! That's my favourite one."

"Your favourite what?"

"My favourite star."

It took me a while to find the one she was pointing at. But sooner or later, there it stood, far from any other, dancing in hues of white and silver.

Not the brightest star mind you, nor by far the biggest, but it was certainly the most peculiar. I could tell why it was her favourite. They were both little lonely dots of silver, her in the ocean, and it in the sky.

"Do you know what it's called?" I asked.

"No, not yet," she said. "I've yet to find out."

Then her little face fell sad, as if she'd

remembered something painful.

"I think it must be terribly lost, all alone in that patch of darkness. No other stars seem to want to go near it. If a star gets too sad, it falls from the sky. So sometimes I light the lighthouse lamp and point it at my star. Just so it knows I'm here. Just so it knows it has a friend."

She fell silent for a moment, admiring the night above, "Stars spend all their time watching us. I think it's only kind that we return the favour sometimes."

Then she turned to me, her look of sadness replaced by sudden excitement, "But you're a grown-up! Surely you know all their names?"

Dear reader, I must confess that I did not. I began to blush with embarrassment, and mumbled something along the lines of "I don't know."

You see, here's one of the things I learned during my time with Tiluna. Something very important, and something I will never fail to forget, that there is absolutely no wisdom without curiosity.

Here I was, a proper grown-up, pretending to know everything about anything. And perhaps I should, grown-ups know a great many important things after all.

But now and then comes along a question of which I do not know the answer to. A question I never thought was worth asking. And why would I? What is the use of knowing the name of every star? I was no astronomer. I had no business knowing such things.

The day we become incurious is the day we become a grown-up. The day we swap our question marks for full stops.

Sometimes I think I grew up too quickly, that little me couldn't wait to be a child no longer. So at far too young an age, I threw away all my notions of being curious, and exchanged all my question marks for full stops. Only once I did that, only once I stopped asking questions, did the grown-ups start calling me a 'good child'.

I'll let you in on a little secret - whenever grown-ups tell you that you're a 'good child', what they actually mean is: 'You'll make a good grown-up.'

Growing old is inevitable, as inevitable as the sun wishing you good morning, and the stars wishing you goodnight. But being curious is always a choice. A choice we give up far too easily.

Those few days with my little friend proved it to me, and perhaps I still had time to fix that. Perhaps we all do.

We sat atop that lonely lighthouse all night, the waves below gently rocking the sea to sleep, as the stars danced above our heads in their thousands.

5

We spent the next three nights putting my boat back together. It was in itself a mismatched mosaic of random things. Of whatever peculiar objects had washed up on Tiluna's shores over the past few years. The sail was made of stitched-up clothes, and the ropes of strengthened seaweed. We worked and worked all throughout the night, only falling asleep when dusk turned into dawn.

When I asked Tiluna why she did this, I said to her, "Is it that you love the stars so much, that you'd rather sleep during the day?"

"What's love?" she replied, whilst making an anchor out of stones.

I wasn't quite sure how to describe it. Everyone has their own definition of love, and I'm sure you've heard many.

"Love is very important," I said. "It's what we can't live without."

These words were not my own of course, someone old had told me that long ago.

"Like food?" Tiluna said.

"Yes, exactly like food," I chuckled. And then the words simply came to me without even thinking of an answer, "Except unlike food, you can *survive* without love, but you can't *live* without love."

"How do you get love?" Tiluna asked. "Where do you find it?"

"Ah that's easy," I said. "Close your eyes, and think of the thing that feels most like home."

Tiluna did so. She sat there for some time.

"What do you see?" I asked her.

"I'm not sure," she whispered. "I don't think I see anything." Tiluna opened her eyes, clearly quite disappointed and confused. "Does that mean I don't have love? Do I not have a home? Am I not living?"

I did my best to reassure her,

"Sometimes, the things we love are standing right in front of us the entire time, and only in their absence can we truly see how much we love them."

I was thinking of home when I said this.

But Tiluna still seemed confused about the whole idea.

"But why do we need it to live? What's so special about love?"

"Well I suppose it's what we live for," I replied. "Love is what we wake up for, and what helps us sleep soundly at night. A life empty of love might lead to a life full of hate."

"And what's hate?" she said. "The opposite of love? If that is so then I hate the day. I hate it, I hate it, I hate it."

"Why do you hate it?"

"Because I don't love it, it has no stars. So I must hate it."

"Oh my little friend," I said shaking my head. "Hate is never the opposite of love. Not caring is the opposite of love. For love and hate are far too strong a feeling to show that you don't care."

"Oh," she said. "Then I don't care much for the day."

6

But it was on the fifth night that tragedy struck. I had woken as usual, just as the day had ended. But Tiluna was nowhere to be found. Not by the boat, not on the rocks, nor anywhere inside the lighthouse itself.

I searched and searched, until at last I found her. She was sat atop the lighthouse lamp, her eyes fixed upon the night above.

But something was troubling her, something was terribly wrong.

"It's gone," she whispered. "My star. It's gone."

"Surely not," I said, as I too peered into the night. But she was right. That little patch of darkness, where only it resided, was darker than ever.

"Do you think-" she mumbled, "do you think it fell from the sky?"

I could see why she thought this. Tiluna hadn't lit the lamp in a long time. She'd been too busy helping me repair my boat.

I tried to reassure her,

"It's the light that's all. It's just not dark enough yet. Your star will come out later, you'll see."

But it did no such thing.

The night passed us by, and that lonely twinkle of silver never showed.

7

And so it was, that on the sixth night, the boat was finally finished. A masterpiece of our own making. Even if a grown-up boatbuilder would say otherwise.

"You can finally go home!" Tiluna said. She smiled a comforting smile, but I think she was still sad about her star. "And although it makes me sad to see you go, I am glad that you are happy. It was nice to have a friend, even for a little while."

In truth, even though I was glad at the thought of home, I felt a twinge of sadness. The thought of leaving this little girl to her lonely lighthouse didn't seem right. But then she said something I did not expect,

"Can I come with you?"

"To England?" I asked.

"To find my star," she said. "If it has fallen from the sky, then it has fallen somewhere here. It's my fault it fell, I should never have left it so sad. I'm supposed to look out for lost things, and, well …"

But she didn't finish her sentence.

"Of course I'll help," I said. It was the least that I could do. I have no doubt that I would be half-drowned if it weren't for Tiluna. Someone told me once that the only way to repay kindness is with kindness itself.

"Promise me we'll find it," she said, as we climbed aboard our little boat. "Promise me we'll bring it home."

"I promise."

And I meant it. I had given her my word. We would search the seas over and over until we found her fallen star.

So it was that we set sail, with not a map nor

compass to guide, with not a destination in mind.

That night we set sail to look out for a lost thing, and to bring it safely home.

8

"So how big is your rock of England?"

We'd been sailing for nearly two days now. Tiluna had sworn that she'd seen a falling star to the west, so to the west was where we sailed.

"Oh England isn't a rock," I chuckled. "It's a country. A big place where lots of people live."

I suppose she must have thought everyone else lived the same way she did, on little islands surrounded by sea.

"And what do people do with their time in England? I know you don't star gaze much."

"Well lots of things. We go to our jobs, we work, we eat, we sleep. And sometimes we do our hobbies when we have time of course."

"Jobs?" she looked confused. "What are they?"

"A job is what you do," I said. "And to some it is your purpose. Your job is a lighthouse keeper, and I imagine you're very good at it."

"But I'm not a lighthouse keeper anymore,"

she replied. "Right now I have no lighthouse to look out from." The thought of this appeared to make her very sad. "What does that make me now? Do I have no purpose?"

"Not at all," I smiled. "Right now, you are an explorer, and a sailor, and by some degree, a scientist."

"What a lot of jobs I have," she smiled. "And what are your jobs? What do you do?"

"Well, I suppose in this moment, I am a sailor, and a friend."

"And what do you enjoy doing?"

I hadn't really thought about this. For the life of me I couldn't remember a single hobby, an interest, or a passing fancy that filled my free time. When I wasn't working, I was sleeping, and when I wasn't sleeping, I was working. Ask any grown-up, and they will tell you that unenjoyable work is very tiring.

"What do you enjoy doing?" she asked again.

It took me a long while to think of an answer. But some little memories came back here and there.

"When I was a child," I said, "I suppose I liked to draw a lot. I wasn't any good at it mind you, and my teachers would always tell me off for doodling in my workbooks. But I enjoyed it all the same."

In truth, the drawings were never anything remarkable, just silly doodles of whatever floated into my head and out through my pencil.

Little silly sketches here and there, of animals in human clothes, and other ridiculous things. Although admittedly they were mostly of my Maths teacher, Mr Simmons, who I liked to draw on account of his *very* bushy moustache.

I will draw a few of them for you here:

"Why don't you draw anymore?" she asked. "Do you not enjoy it?"

Of course, I didn't want to tell Tiluna the real reason. The real reason was that I didn't think I'd be successful, or more importantly, the grown-ups told me that I wouldn't be successful.

My little doodles were nothing like the great paintings that hung in those dusty art galleries. My silly little sketches had no place in the eyes of the serious art critics, and the grown-ups made sure to tell me so.

So I threw away my drawing pens. I left my sketchbooks to gather dust on some long-forgotten shelf, and I became a serious grown-up like them.

"Oh, I was just never any good at art," I mumbled. That wasn't true of course, but it was a very grown-up answer.

Tiluna thought to herself for a little while, before saying,

"Maybe being good at something isn't the point of it."

"What do you mean?"

"Well before this week, I'd never sailed a boat, but now I know that I enjoy it immensely. I'm not as good as you, but I enjoy it all the same."

I suppose most grown-ups have this idea that you can only do something if you are that certain something. If you are a painter, then you paint. If you are a singer, then you sing. But what most grown-ups don't understand, is that they have it completely the wrong way around.

If you sing, no matter how badly, then you are a singer. If you paint, no matter how terribly, then you are a painter. Children on the other hand, understand this perfectly. When they want to paint, they paint. When they want to sing, they sing. They certainly do not wait until they have become a painter or a singer to do so.

I wonder how many lifetimes have been wasted with the absence of 'what if?'

"What would you do," I asked Tiluna, "if you had the chance to do anything?"

She seemed rather confused by this.

"Well if I had the chance to do anything," she said, "I suppose I'd like to do everything. Yes. I'd very much like to do a bit of everything."

9

But the calm autumn skies did not last long, and one night our patchwork boat was engulfed by a furious thunderstorm. The same thunderstorm I dare say that led me to Tiluna's lighthouse.

The thunder rocked our boat this way and that, the little vessel barely fighting to keep afloat against the angry waves.

Then, between one flash of lightning and the next, part of our boat snapped clean off, sending Tiluna tumbling down into the violent sea.

I called out her name, I yelled and yelled until my voice was all but sore. But answer there came none.

Rest assured dear reader, I did eventually find Tiluna, but only after many sleepless nights of searching. And those nights were so sad and so hopeless, that I won't dare write them down here.

Instead, I shall share the stories of her own little adventures, and of what she found far out to sea.

10

Tiluna had drifted for so far, and for so long, that the storm was nothing more than a bunch of angry clouds on the horizon.

Sat atop a piece of driftwood, she took off her scarf and wrapped it around a makeshift mast, so that her boat would have a sail.

"There," she smiled. "Now I'm an engineer as well."

And so she sailed, on and on, over sea and under sky.

That night she thought of her silver star. How alone it must be right now, how scared it must feel without her lighthouse lamp to keep it company.

She searched and searched the night above, for that little hope of silver. But no matter how hard she looked, she still could not find it, and it could not find her.

And for the first time in her life, Tiluna understood what it was to be lonely.

"Oh my silver star," she whispered into the night. "The more I try to forget you, the more I miss you so."

11

You won't be surprised to hear that there are lots of little islands in the world, many of which still haven't been found by explorers.

You'll be familiar with the big ones I'm sure, as most modern maps proudly display their names so that you don't forget them.

When you next look at a map of the world, you'll notice the very big islands like 'Australia' or 'America'.

These are labelled in such big letters because grown-ups think the bigger the island the more important it must be.

But as many named islands as there are, there are an equal number of unnamed ones. Modern cartographers think these islands too small and too insignificant to bother putting them on the map.

"What a waste of ink," they'd say if you ever brought it up, and carry on filling in the big islands like Australia or America.

But these little islands, often missed out in our world maps, are home to a number of people nonetheless.

And so it was that Tiluna found herself adrift, sailing from one small island to the other. Curious of what she might find. Curious about the world of grown-ups.

Perhaps they would help her find her star.

12

The first island that Tiluna came to was very small indeed. As if a mighty tall grown-up could cross to the other side in one step.

A big proportion of the little rock was taken up by a magnificent wooden desk, behind which sat a large balding man. His swollen sausage-like fingers greedily hammered away at a calculator, whilst his other hand entered these numbers on a great big computer.

"Excuse me," she said to the man, "have you seen a falling star nearby?"

But he made no answer, and continued to press the buttons on his calculator.

"Excuse me," she repeated, "have you-"

"Do you have an appointment?" mumbled the merchant.

"Um. No, no not quite," Tiluna said. "I was just sailing past-"

"Well you need an appointment," he said cutting her off. "I'm a busy man."

Tiluna looked around the little rock, but not a soul save the two of them were there.

"I don't see anyone else here," she said.

The merchant grumbled, and waved a dismissive hand, still not looking up from his desk.

"What do you do for a living?" he asked.

"I look out for lost things," she said. "I look out from my lighthouse every night."

"What a waste of time," he grumbled. "Not much money to be made there."

Time. That was the thing with the wristwatch. But the merchant's wristwatch was far shinier than her lost friends. Maybe that meant he had more time. Her friend did say they didn't have time to go star gazing in the evenings. Perhaps grown-ups just need more time.

Just as she was about to ask him how much time he had, the merchant spoke,

"A lighthouse though, valuable property no doubt. How many islands do you own?"

"Just one," said Tiluna. "I have my lighthouse. But I don't think I own it …"

"You should sell it," the merchant interrupted. "Then you can buy two more islands."

"Why would I do that?"

"So you can wait for them to go up in value, and then sell them, so you can buy four more islands."

"But I like my island," she said. "It's all I need. I wouldn't know what to do with four islands. I can't possibly be on four islands all at once."

But the merchant didn't listen to this, still hunched over his computer and calculator.

"Yes, yes," he mumbled dismissively. "Well if you do want to sell, here's my card."

He brandished a thin piece of paper at her, still not looking up from his desk. "Now I'm a busy man, and my time is precious, so if you don't mind."

What a waste of time, Tiluna thought to herself. To have all that time, and to spend it in such a silly way.

13

The second island was much bigger than the first, but contained only half of what the merchants had. A man in paint-stained overalls stood before an easel. His face so consumed with decision-making, that his eyebrows looked as if they might take flight any second.

"What are you doing?" asked Tiluna.

"I'm painting," moaned the artist. But the canvas was bare. No paint, no pencil marks, nothing to do with art whatsoever.

"What are you painting?"

"I haven't decided yet," said the artist.

"Why don't you paint the sky?" she proposed.

"Hmm," mumbled the artist, "I could do …"

"It's very pretty this time of night," said Tiluna. "Maybe paint the moon? Or the stars?"

"Yes, yes I suppose …"

After a moment of thoughtful silence, the artist said,

"But I'm not sure which one to paint. Which do you think is more beautiful? The moon? Or the stars? Which will sell better?"

But Tiluna didn't know the answer, so she simply said,

"I think the moon and stars are far from similar. Yet both are unmatched in their beauty. I think comparison ruins beautiful things."

"Yes, yes. That's all *very* well. But which will *sell* better."

She didn't quite understand the artist. Maybe he just needed more time. He had no wristwatch after all.

"If you want a shinier watch to get more time, why don't you become a merchant? I know a merchant." She reached into her pocket to take out his card, and held it up to the artist.

"No no, dear child, you simply don't understand. I paint because I want to be a painter! And I'm determined to make a living from doing so."

But he was still comparing the moon and stars as he said this.

14

One night Tiluna woke to find her boat had drifted very close to shore. Great stone cliffs stretched up and up, until they all but disappeared into the grey clouds above. There seemed no way around them, nor anyway over.

She had half a mind to sail on pass, when she spotted a person standing at the bottom of the cliffs, gazing up at the towering heights above her.

"Hello," said Tiluna.

"Hello," replied the woman, her eyes still fixed on something up above. She was wearing very funny clothes. Her hands were covered in chalk, and on her head sat a very thick helmet.

"What are you looking at?" Tiluna asked, trying to follow her gaze.

"A better way up," the climber replied.

"Up this cliff?" Tiluna said surprised. "Surely there's no way up something that high?"

"Maybe not," the climber replied. "But I've been trying all the same. After all, there's only one way to find out."

Tiluna gulped as she looked at the sheer height of the thing. The thought of climbing that was beginning to make her very dizzy indeed.

She was used to being high up, having spent a great many nights sat atop her lighthouse. But this cliff was something else entirely. Surely no one could climb that.

"How many times have you tried?" Tiluna asked the Climber.

"Oh, I've lost count …" she chuckled, "definitely more than most."

"And you failed every time?"

"Every time," she smiled.

"Aren't you afraid you'll fail again?"

"So what if I do?" the climber said. "I've failed before, and I'll fail again. I'll keep on failing until I get it right."

"Doesn't it hurt when you fall back down?"

"Of course it does," she said. "But I'd rather sit atop the cliff having failed a thousand times, than stand sadly at the bottom never having tried."

15

The next island was so incredibly small, that it didn't have space for two fully grown grown-ups to sit. A man with shiny skin was lounging on a long comfortable sofa, his hair neatly combed and well-kept. He clearly had no room for company.

"Am I not beautiful?" said the muse.

"I can't say," replied Tiluna, "I don't know you yet."

"No no child," he chuckled. "My appearance, am I not the most beautiful person you have ever seen."

"I know an artist," she said. "Perhaps he would like to paint you one day."

"I'm sure he would!" the muse grinned, with a smile that didn't quite reach his eyes. "He would be *very* lucky to paint me."

"Why?"

"Because my body is *perfect.* I have no marks, no scars, no blemishes, and I look far younger than I actually am."

Tiluna was rather puzzled by this,

"What's wrong with marks? I think the

marks on our bodies are quite useful actually."

"I beg your pardon?" said the muse, rather taken aback.

"Well I think the marks on our bodies tell us a story where words cannot."

He looked quite shocked, as if she had told him something terribly rude and nasty.

"See these," Tiluna said, showing him the palms of her hands. "These rope burns tell the world that I am a sailor, that I have many interesting stories to tell about my times at sea."

"How ridiculous," said the muse. "You should moisturise those burns, they look ugly."

"So what stories do you have?" Tiluna asked.

"I beg your pardon?"

"What stories do you have?" she repeated. "Have you ever moved from your sofa?"

"Of course I haven't," he snapped back. "I stay here so I can keep myself from scars, to keep myself perfect in every way."

What an odd thing to do, Tiluna thought to herself, what an odd way to spend your time.

"Well I think a perfect body without these scars has never truly lived," she said. "Like a scar upon your leg from where you've been climbing, or those furrowed marks across your brow that show you've been smiling. Those laughter lines that show of all the times you were alive. A perfect body without these marks has never truly lived. I think our bodies tell a story where words cannot."

"Well then," said the muse, "you shall grow to be a very *ugly* grown-up. And I can't be seen in the company of *ugly* people. Goodbye."

Tiluna thought quietly to herself as she sailed away, that people are neither ugly nor beautiful, not until you get to know them.

And how ugly that muse was. He would make a very good painting, that's for sure. But all his beauty was just for the eyes to see. That when he came to speak, he was entirely hollow inside.

16

The next island was inhabited by a very peculiar grown-up indeed. A curious fellow, with goggles for eyes, hunched over his little wooden workbench. He appeared to be working on something very small and complicated.

DING! A little noise cried out.

"What's that noise?" Tiluna asked.

The watchmaker glanced at the thing on his wrist, and muttered under his breath,

"Dear me, I'm late for dinner."

He reached into his pocket without further ado and pulled out a small cereal bar. He devoured the thing in less than five whole seconds, his personal best!

DING! Went the little watch again.

"What time is it now?" Tiluna asked.

"Back to work time!" he flustered, and sat back down at his workbench. He clearly had no time to pause and think.

"What are those noises?" she asked of the busy man.

DING!
"What noises?" he said.

DING!
"Oh those noises!" he held up his wrist, and showed Tiluna the watch.

"It tells the time," he said. "And more importantly, it tells me how long I have left to do something. It's dreadfully bad business to run out of time you know."

"You can run out of time?"

"Why of course!" he said in a fluster. "There

are only so many moments in a day. But with this watch, a person can carefully plan and track their entire life to the nearest second!"

The little watch went DING yet again, signalling that it was time to do something else.

"Your entire life?" Tiluna said. "You know what you'll be doing for the rest of your entire life?"

"Why yes indeed," he replied. "But sometimes, on a good day, I do things a great deal quicker than planned. So I have extra time to spare!"

"And what do you do with your spare time?"

DING!

"Dear me! Time flies!" declared the watchmaker, as he set about doing another task.

"What do you do with your spare time?" Tiluna asked again.

DING! DING! DING!

"Oh dear," mumbled the watchmaker. "I didn't schedule this conversation, I'm thirty seconds into my sleeping time. Goodnight!"

And with that, he rested his head upon the

workbench, and began to softly snore.

'What a stressful life,' Tiluna thought to herself. She had no idea time was so precious. She'd thought time was like the night and day, that the sun may set, but we'd always have another tomorrow. Could you really run out of it? What if she ran out of time?

Time flies, that was what the watchmaker had said. But what did he mean by it?

"Time flies …" she whispered softly into the night, contemplating the oddness of it all.

And so there she stood, beside the sea for quite a while, admiring the crows as they danced up above.

"Time flies," she whispered, as the wind whispered also.

"Time flies," she whispered, as her eyes lit up with the light of a thousand stars.

"Time flies," she whispered, as the crows danced and danced.

"Time flies," she whispered, and time, for that moment, stood perfectly still.

Tiluna smiled, and looked up to the sky, to that little patch of dark where once she knew her star to be.

"Oh my lonely star," she said. "Time is very

cruel, I wish we had more time. The lonely hours not spent with you were wasted hours of mine."

17

The next island was barely even visible. Great stacks of books lay there one on top of the other. Ginormous tomes of very important matters, all huddled for space on that little floating rock.

And there, nestled between them, sat an old man with wizened white hair. His neatly trimmed beard mumbled up and down, as he followed the words in the book between his hands.

"What are these?" asked Tiluna.

"These are books," he mumbled, not looking up from his.

"And what do you do with them?"

He stared at Tiluna, as if she had asked a very silly question.

"You *read* them," he said.

"Why do you read them?"

"Because I am a philosopher," he mumbled, stroking his neatly trimmed beard. "I read a great many books. Now if you don't mind, I have some reading to get back to. Good day."

"What are you reading?" Tiluna asked, trying to make sense of the strange words on the front of his book.

"Something very important, and no doubt something very difficult for a child to understand. Good day."

"What does a philosopher do exactly? Do they just read all day?"

He looked up from his book, and sighed impatiently,

"No child, don't be absurd. No one can make a living from reading all day."

"So what does a philosopher do?"

He sighed once more and twirled his

wizened moustache.

"A philosopher, which I am, ponders the meaning of life."

"There's a meaning to life?" Tiluna was rather taken aback. First we had to count our time, and now life has a meaning? Grown-ups really are quite odd. What silly things they come up with.

"Well of course there is! Silly girl," he said as he snapped the book shut, and readjusted his spectacles. "The trouble is, we philosophers can't decide on which meaning."

"There's more than one meaning!?"

"Of course there is!" he sneered. "Too many if you ask me."

Then Tiluna had a thought, and really quite a good idea,

"Why don't you put all the meanings into a hat, and pick one at random?"

But the philosopher just laughed, "Oh the ignorance of youth," he chortled. "Now good day, I must get back to reading. I have an important day tomorrow."

"Why is it important?" she said.

The philosopher just sighed.

"Because I'm taking an exam."

An exam? Those sounded odd whatever they were.

"What's an exam?" she asked.

The philosopher was getting rather impatient now.

"An exam," he sighed with gritted teeth, "is a day in which you prove that you know things."

"So why is it important?"

He huffed a great huff, and told Tiluna,

"Because I need to know everything in this book, or I won't be taken seriously by all the other philosophers."

He reopened it, and riffled back to the page he was on, "That is why it is an important day, and today I am sat here talking to you, which makes it a very *unimportant* day!"

The philosopher readjusted his spectacles once more, and immersed himself in reading, "Now goodbye," he said as he waved a dismissive hand.

"Well," Tiluna said, "I think either every day is an important day, or none of them are."

"And what would a little child know of such things? Hm? How many exams have you taken?"

"Well, none, but-"

"Ah well there you have it! I am much older than you, and therefore much wiser. I have several exams that say so."

What a rude thing to say.

"I don't think that age equals wisdom," she said. "I think that some learn more in one year than others do in twenty. I know a man who does nothing but sit on his sofa all day, thinking that curiosity will make him ugly! But he doesn't know a thing! And he's a grown-up!"

But she received no reply, and there was a silence between them.

Then a thought came to her,

"Can you help me find my star? Perhaps you've read about finding stars in one of your books?"

"I'm a philosopher," he said. "Not an astronomer. Good day."

Tiluna said no more, and left the philosopher to his reading.

18

It was soon that Tiluna found herself on a very empty island. No grown-ups, no trees, nothing but little groups of butterflies dancing on the breeze.

"I know you!" she said, holding out her hand. "You're a butterfly!"

"That I am!" said one of purest blue and purple. "And what are you may I ask?"

"I'm Tiluna," she said. "Or at least I think I used to be."

"Used to be?" said the butterfly. "Well then, who are you now?"

"I'm not so sure anymore," she replied. "I think I have changed a great deal since I left home."

"Ah!" said the butterfly. "So you were once a caterpillar too!"

"No not quite," Tiluna giggled. "Or at least I don't think so. I just feel less of myself that's all. Yes, I think I've become less of myself, I feel somehow changed."

"We don't become any less of ourselves," said the butterfly, as it danced in the wind.

"Even though we all change, every moment of every day. Why look at me! Just a few days ago I was a different thing entirely, but still here I am.

So whoever you think you are now and whatever you have done, is always going to be greater than what came before. For we are what came before, and everything more. We don't become any less of ourselves."

19

And so Tiluna sailed, from this dawn to the next, doing what all great explorers do. A great explorer makes a habit of constantly staying curious. For an explorer who thinks they know everything has nothing to explore.

Tiluna had sailed for so far, and for so long, that she had quite forgotten which way was west and which way was east. Up was now down, and down had become up. Finding your way can be so confusing when all you see is water.

Every morning she would go to sleep in the hope of her star returning. That perhaps this night, just as she would wake, she would search the sky above and see that little hope of silver. That the worst hadn't happened after all, that it had never fallen from the sky.

But no matter how many times she woke, no matter how many times she went to sleep with hope in her heart, she still could not find it. Perhaps it really was gone forever.

The longer she spent adrift, the more she doubted herself. The world was much wider than she thought, and the sea much more endless than she'd ever imagined.

She never knew just how much her star meant to her. She never knew how lonely she would be without it. Those many nights spent staring at each other, those two little lights of silver.

And although they often spent their time in silence, their company brought each other a sense of friendship where a thousand conversations could not.

A friendship like that is hard to come by. But when you find it, it's the most beautiful thing in the world. More beautiful I dare say, than a thousand sunsets at sea.

20

Soon after she found herself floating near the island of a murmuring woman. She was sat quite still, upon a rickety wooden stool. A great long telescope pressed up to her unclosed eye.

"326B2, 326B3, 326B4 …" the woman counted on and on.

"What are you doing?" Tiluna asked her.
But she made no reply, and carried on with her counting.
"326B5, 326B6 …"
"What are you doing?" she politely asked again.

"326B – oh bother!" the woman cried out. "Look what you've made me do! Now I shall have to start all over again."

"Start over with what?"

"326B2, 326B3 …"

"Start over with what?"

"Oh what's the use!" she cried, as she flung her arms up in resignation.

"What's the use with what?"

"I'm naming the stars," said the woman, making a note of her progress. "And you're interrupting me!"

Tiluna glanced at her notebook. It was filled with a great many numbers, yet strangely there appeared no names.

"You name the stars?" Tiluna asked.

Finally! Here was a grown-up worth talking to! This was a very good use of time indeed.

"Yes, I'm an astronomer," she said. "It is my business to name the stars."

"What were those numbers you were calling out? Are you adding something up?"

"No, no," the astronomer said as a matter of fact. "Those are their names. The names of every star. I name them as I see them."

"But those aren't names!" Tiluna giggled.

"Names are unique, numbers are just numbers!"

"Be that as it may," she said, "I have no time to find unique names for each and every star. If I did my job would take twice as long!"

Tiluna was beginning to think that she had judged her a little too quickly.

"But that's not very nice," she said. "If you name them in numbers, then they're not unique in the slightest."

The astronomer looked rather puzzled, and said,

"That's because stars are *not* unique."

"What do you mean?"

"Well," she murmured, "they all look the same from here. If you were walking along a beach, you wouldn't name every grain of sand you come across now would you."

Tiluna pretended not to hear her. What she was saying wasn't very nice. How would you feel if you were nothing more than a string of numbers? Quite replaceable I'm sure.

Then a thought came to her. Here was a grown-up, whose business it was to know about stars.

"Please," she said, "if you are an

astronomer, please help me find my star."

"*Your* star?"

"Yes, my star."

The astronomer scratched her chin in thought, "How can someone lose a star?"

"It's not where it usually is," Tiluna said. "It's gone from the sky."

"Hmm," pondered the astronomer. "Well I'm afraid I can't help you there … why don't you pick a new one. They're all the same after all. It will save you a lot of time and bother."

"But it's *my* star," she said. "I don't want another. It wouldn't be the same."

The astronomer said no more on the matter, and returned to her telescope,

"326B4, 326B5, 326B6 …"

Tiluna sailed away a great deal sadder than when she had found her.

What if the astronomer was right? What if her star wasn't that special at all? What if it was just a singular number among the many same around it? Nothing more than a grain of sand on a nearly endless beach.

She looked up to the sky, and thought about choosing a new one. It was true, they were nearly all identical in appearance. They were all very beautiful, even the struggling artist would agree on that.

But they all felt so dull and boring compared to hers.

And they didn't look quite so lonely.

21

A sculptor stood before her statue, hammer and chisel in hand. It was such a beautiful thing, and yet the sculptor seemed thoroughly unimpressed with her work.

"Hmmm," mumbled the sculptor. "Not quite perfect." And she proceeded to smash the statue into little tiny pieces.

"Why did you do that?" Tiluna asked.

"It wasn't perfect in the slightest," replied the sculptor. "My work *has* to be perfect."

Tiluna looked around the island, and there lay nothing but fragments of smashed-up statues.

"How many times have you created something just to destroy it?"

"Oh a thousand times at least," she said.

"None of my statues have been perfect. But maybe the next one will."

"But how do you know they're not perfect? You never finish them! You smash them up before they're ever completed."

"Because I can tell before they're finished!" the sculptor said. "If I finish them, people will know that I'm not good at sculpting. And then people will judge me for not being the best sculptor. I have to be the best, I have to be better than them!"

What an odd way to live.

"Surely it should never really matter if you are not better than them," Tiluna said. "You'll never grow that way. Surely all that matters is that you are better than who you were yesterday."

But the sculptor said nothing, and got to work on her next block of marble.

What a waste of work, Tiluna thought to herself. That striving for perfection does nothing but harm your chances of creating it.

22

The faint sound of ringing bells floated from far away. It was coming from a very tiny island indeed, no bigger than a wisp of clouds. But this island was different to the rest. It had no rocks, no sand, no grass. It was, in itself, as plain as plain can be. And there, dancing slowly in the light of dawn, was a sad little jester.

"Good morning, good evening, good day, and good morrow," he sang mournfully. "The day that we part will be a day full of sorrow."

"I'm sorry?" said Tiluna. "What do you mean, good morning, good evening and good day? Surely it can't be all of them at once."

"Can it not?" replied the sad jester, as he ceased his prancing and dancing. "Well it might as well be one of them, so why can't it be all of them."

"You're wearing very funny clothes," said Tiluna, nearing a giggle.

"That's because I'm a jester," he said. "I'm supposed to be funny."

"What's a jester?"

"A person who laughs at everything. That is my job," he said with a smile that didn't quite reach his eyes.

"You don't seem too happy about it."

"That's because I have to be funny *all* the time, and sometimes I can't be."

"And why do grown-ups need jesters? I thought they were all very serious?"

"Grown-ups need jesters, because sometimes the world gets *too* serious. They need jesters to remind them that if we cannot laugh at something, then it still has power over us."

Grown-ups are so peculiar, Tiluna thought to herself. They have specific times to be serious, and specific times to be unserious.

"If your job is to laugh at everything," said Tiluna, "then why are you so sad?"

"Because I am a jester, and yet I have no audience. A good jester needs an audience."

"Can't you be happy without an audience?"

"Of course not," he mumbled, shuffling a deck of cards. "I am supposed to be a funny person, I make people laugh. And I can't make people laugh when they're not here! I need my audience to function, without them I am not a complete person."

This confused Tiluna very much. Here was a grown-up who was doing what he loved, and yet it made him so terribly miserable. That all his laughter lines were from fake smiles.

"Well, if you can't be yourself without an audience," she said, "then surely you're not a person, surely you're just a character, like someone in a book. Aren't you tired of acting all the time?"

But he didn't answer, instead, he pulled out some more cards and continued to practice his magic tricks.

23

After the island of the sad jester, Tiluna saw an otter swimming happily between the waves. Its tail dancing to and fro with every swish and swash from the sea.

"What an odd sort of boat you have," said the otter. "Are you a fisherman?"

"I'm a lighthouse keeper," said Tiluna, but

then quickly remembered, "I'm also a sailor, I'm an astronomer and just recently I became an engineer."

"How interesting!" replied the otter. "Because I only ever meet fishermen out here, and they usually try and catch me in their nets."

"Why would they want to catch you? You're not a fish. Are you?"

"No no," the otter chuckled, "I'm not a fish! I don't know why they chase after me … but I've never thought it a good idea to stop and ask."

Tiluna thought that sounded rather sensible.

"Well, how did you know that I wouldn't try to catch you? I could have been a fisherman after all."

The otter just shrugged,

"I took a chance," he said. "I must admit that I was very scared, but there's always something beautiful on the other side of fear. Because now I think I've met a good friend. I have always wanted a friend."

"As have I," smiled Tiluna. "I only have my star, but I can't seem to find it anymore."

"A star?" said the otter. "How does a person

make friends with a star?"

"I keep it company every night," she said, "as all the other ones seem to have friends close by."

"How do you keep a star company?"

"With my lighthouse lamp. Every night I shine its light right at my silver star, so it knows it's not alone. So it knows it has a friend."

Then a thought crossed her mind, one she had been thinking about for a long time. "Will you come and live with me in my lighthouse? Because I think I am very lonely up there, and I am in need of a friend."

"Ah, I'm afraid I can't," said the otter. "For I belong in the sea. I wouldn't be very happy high up in a lighthouse."

"Even if you had a friend with you?"

"Even if I had a friend with me."

Tiluna's little face fell sad when she heard this.

"But that doesn't mean we can't be friends now," the otter smiled.

"Then what is the point in making friends," said Tiluna, "if all friendships must someday end?"

"Everything ends," replied the otter. "There is no denying that. But some things, like a beautiful friendship, are worth the tearful ending."

"And will you cry a lot when we are no longer friends?"

"Of course," said the otter. "But that is not such a bad thing. Tears are where memories go when they don't want to be forgotten."

"I don't think I'll ever want to forget a friend," said Tiluna.

"Then someday you will cry, and I will cry too. But at least that way we shall never forget each other. At least that way we'll always be friends."

And so they sailed on into the dawn, the otter and the lighthouse keeper. Two unlikely friends, asleep in each other's arms.

Tiluna and the otter travelled together for a great many days. It was good to have a friend again.

After spending some time on the islands of grown-ups, she found that being alone is far from loneliness. But to be surrounded by those that make you feel alone, is a loneliness in itself. But now she had a friend, a friend that made one friendship feel like a thousand, and because of that loneliness would never take hold.

And in those precious few days with her newfound friend, she laughed and laughed. Perhaps more than she ever had all those years atop her lonely lighthouse.

Their friendship saw them through calm autumn nights, and endured terrible storms that shook the very sea itself. But no storm was ever permanent, and no clear sky lasted forever.

"For as long as you are here my friend," the otter would often say, "we'll sail this storm together. For we who learn to sail the storm can master any weather."

He often said odd things like that. He was, after all, quite an odd otter. But the most interesting things often are peculiar in some way or another. It is far, far better to be bonkers than boring.

The grown-ups that she'd met hadn't been peculiar at all, in fact, they seemed to despise the idea. They were all very sensible thank you very much, or at least, sensible in a grown-up sort of way.

"I have a feeling you'll be leaving me soon," said Tiluna one day. "For you seem very sad."

"I'm homesick," replied the otter. "I'm homesick and I miss my home."

It had been a great many days since Tiluna had been home.

"I understand," she said, even though she didn't want to.

"But I want you to know something," said the otter, "something very important."

The otter made sure Tiluna was listening very carefully, and then he softly spoke,

"When I'm gone, I'll just be a memory in your head. But that's okay, for as long as it makes you smile, then that is all I could ever wish for. Tears are where memories go when they don't want to be forgotten. We're all just memories in the end. I hope that I'll be a good one."

Then one night Tiluna woke to find the otter had gone. She wasn't surprised, she had been prepared for such a goodbye. But being prepared for something doesn't make it any less hurtful. And in that moment, she discovered something very painful about loving someone. That the hardest goodbyes are the ones which are never said.

And no matter how hard you love something, no matter how much it means to you, you must always let it go in the end.

I think she began to understand what love truly was. That love is rarely realised when it's right in front of us, but when it's far, far away.

24

The departure of her friend had left Tiluna so very sad. But although they may never meet again, she was glad to have someone to miss. Missing someone means that you loved them truly.

And it was in times like these that her thoughts turned to her lonely star. She wondered if it too had ever lost someone it loved. That if it too felt as lonely as she did now.

That perhaps, where now there was empty sky, maybe there once were many silver stars like it. How cold it must have felt, all alone high up in that dark sky, when it no longer felt the warmth of her lighthouse lamp. No wonder stars fall down when they are sad.

It was certainly very fun being an explorer, and a sailor, and a great many other things. But she had to find her silver star, she had to find her friend, fallen or not.

She had made a promise.

25

But no matter how hard she searched, no matter how long she sailed the sea over and over, her star was nowhere to be found.

So on and on her makeshift boat drifted, until the waters became cold, and the nights even colder. Large chunks of floating ice began to cover the freezing waves, and animals of the most bizarre kind dwelt there.

"What strange hair you have," said a polar bear as she passed him by.

"Thank you," said Tiluna. "It's like my star."

This was one of the very first compliments she had ever received. All the grown-ups she'd met seemed so obsessed with themselves. Far too busy to be curious enough to pay someone else a compliment.

"You're not like the other people I've seen sailing around these waters," the polar bear said. "They looked much older, and much more tired."

"Why? Who have you seen sailing around here?" She was hoping that he had seen her lost grown-up from England. She was hoping that he had seen me.

"Fishermen," the polar bear glumly mumbled. "But I do my best to avoid them."

"My friend was hunted by fishermen. Do they come and hunt you too?"

"Sometimes," said the polar bear. "But not to eat me mind you."

"Then why do they hunt you?"

"Because some people, for whatever reason, like to be cruel."

"Why?"

"I think it makes them feel courageous."

"Well, I think they're cowards," said Tiluna.

"Of course," replied the polar bear. "There is cowardness in cruelty, and courage in kindness, and yet we never fail to mix these up."

"I'll be kind to you," she said. "I like the sound of being courageous, whatever that is."

"That's very thoughtful of you," chuckled the polar bear. "But true kindness is kind because it expects no reward."

"I don't suppose you've seen my friend?" Tiluna asked, not knowing how to cheer up the polar bear.

"The one hunted by fishermen?"

"No, no sorry, the other one. They're a grown-up."

The polar bear raised his furry head, and

scratched his chin with his paw, "Hmm, I can't say that it was definitely them. Mind you, lots of grown-ups pass through, taking bits of ice here and there."

"How come?"

"I suppose they don't have enough ice back home," he glumly mumbled. "So they come and take mine. They're very greedy like that."

"I'm sorry," she said.

Tiluna had learnt a great deal since leaving her lonely lighthouse, but of everything she had found, of everything she had discovered, the nature of grown-ups was the thing she liked the least. How dull their world seemed, so full of mechanical minds. The merchant, the artist, the muse, the astronomer, the watchmaker, the jester, the philosopher, the sculptor, all of them had achieved a great many things. But of all their great achievements, none of them were kind.

"You seem very sad," Tiluna said to the polar bear. "How do you live with sadness?"

But the polar bear didn't reply at first, he was just thinking, and staring out to sea.

Then at last, he spoke.

"My mother told me once, that I should

admire every sunset as if it were to be my last. For no amount of sadness can numb nature's beauty."

Then he smiled softly, "I'll tell your grown-up that you passed through here, if they ever do the same."

The polar bear was kind, thought Tiluna. So very kind. In his heart he held all that sadness, and yet it only made him kinder. Kindness is the only achievement ever worth striving for. And yet it seems to be the one grown-ups are least concerned with.

26

That night she lay on her makeshift boat and cried until her eyes were sore. What a bleak world of grown-ups she had found, what an awful way in which grown-ups spent what little time they had. She feared that she would never get home, that she would never see her lighthouse again.

Not only was she lonely as lonely can be, but now she had become the very thing she was supposed to look out for, she had become a lost thing.

So she did what anyone would do in the face of feeling lost. She closed her eyes, and thought very hard of home.

Home. Oh how she wished to see home once more. Her lighthouse, her silver star, the way the sun set over the sea.

Home was wherever she could see her star.

Oh how she missed her silver star.

She never knew how much it meant to her, not until it had gone for good. She never knew just how much she'd loved it. Oh how she would give anything to see it one last time.

"Are you alright?" came a grumbling voice from behind.

And there, sat comfortably in a little green boat, was a fisherman.

He was a big, odd-looking man, with a bird's nest for a beard and two hedgerows for a brow.

The shaggy brown hair that topped his head shot out in all directions, as if a bolt of lightning was permanently imminent.

If you were to bump into him on the street, you might say that he looked very old, or very stressed, possibly both.

"Are you alright?" he mumbled again. Tiluna thought he had a very funny voice. It sounded like a rolling thunder, and yet had the charm of a song.

"Yes, yes, sorry," she said, wiping the tears from her eyes. "I'm lost, that's all."

"Well now," said the man, his great bushy beard mumbling up and down as he spoke, "that's not a thing to be sorry about. Where are you headed?"

"My star," she mumbled. "I'm looking for my star."

"Fallen from the sky has it?"

"Yes, yes exactly!" Finally, a grown-up who understood!

"Terrible shame that," he said. His soft thunderous voice was so soothing.

But still Tiluna was wary of the man. And quite right too. For he was a fisherman, and her friends did not like fishermen.

"Are you looking for fish?" she asked.

"That I am," he smiled. "Have you ever been fishing before?"

Tiluna shook her head.

"Ah, you're missing out!" he grinned. "Come, I'll show you how."

Tiluna tied her raft to the little green boat, and the two sat there for some time, enjoying the morning sun.

He showed her how to cast, and how to

attach food to the hook. They sat for a while in silence, occasionally pulling the bait from the waters, but they hadn't caught anything yet.

"This star," the fisherman said. "Was it a good friend of yours?"

"Yes," she mumbled. "My oldest friend. I have known it all my life. I love it very much. But I didn't know how much until I lost it."

The fisherman smiled, a warm smile that reached his wrinkled old eyes.

"But that's for the better? No? Now you know how much it means to you, now you know how much you love it. And when you find it again, it'll be the best feeling in the world."

Tiluna smiled half-heartedly, the other half of her heart still full of doubt.

It had been some time since the storm had cleared, and a rainbow had formed upon the horizon.

"How lovely," said Tiluna.

"How lovely," said the fisherman.

"I wonder," he said, "if we'd truly appreciate the beauty of rainbows, if it didn't rain before."

28

They sat there for some time, watching the day go by. Sometimes a good day is a day in which nothing is done at all. Grown-ups enjoy these days very much.

But soon something stirred in the waters below, a gentle ripple that came from the sea.

They reeled in their fishing line, but again they'd had caught nothing.

"Have you ever lost someone?" Tiluna asked. "Like I lost my star?"

The fisherman seemed to understand a great deal, maybe once he had a star like hers.

"Yes," he said, smiling gently. "I expect most people have. But that's the condition of loving someone. And I lost her a long time ago."

But just as he was about to continue, the fishing rod lurched forward, as if the very sea itself was pulling it down.

"Quickly!" the fisherman yelled with excitement. "Grab the rod! Quickly now!"

They pulled and pulled. It was quite the battle. Whatever was on the other end had clearly done this many times before.

They pulled and pulled with all their might, until the fish finally flew from the water.

"Great bulbous barnacles!" cried the fisherman. "Look at the size of that one!"

Tiluna giggled at the sound of his voice. The fish soared up and up into the air, and then landed in the boat by their feet.

It was magnificent, a mosaic of all the splendid colours. Tiluna had never seen a fish like it in all her life.

"Beautiful, ain't he," the fisherman mumbled, picking it up in his hairy hands for her to see.

"Are you going to keep him?" she asked.

"I'd very much like to," he said. "Just look at his scales, how magnificent! I'd love to put him on display, in a big old water tank in my house. So that I could see just how beautiful he is every day."

He paused for a moment, admiring the creature in his hands,

"But a thing isn't beautiful because you have it forever. It's beautiful because you know you might not see it again. All moments must pass for them to be memorable at all."

And with that, he gently placed the fish back into the sea.

Tiluna thought of her star. Had all their moments together passed as well? Would she ever see it again?

"Do you miss her?" she said. "Do you miss your friend?"

The mere thought of her made the fisherman smile so warmly. It was as if she were sitting there right beside him.

He didn't need to say anything, Tiluna understood perfectly. Sometimes no words are ever enough to describe a feeling. Sometimes silence is the perfect answer.

"You must have been very good friends," she said.

"Oh Tiluna," he smiled. "You should have met her. I tell you, no time was better spent than the time I spent with her. I don't regret a second of it, and I wouldn't change a minute neither."

How happy he seemed, just at the thought of his friend. Soon his thoughts had turned to tears, and they rolled gently down his cheek.

"Do you think you'll see her again?" Tiluna asked. "In another life perhaps?"

The fisherman chuckled.

"I dearly hope so," he said as he wiped away the tear. "But I know one thing for sure, there's no afterlife worth dying for, if it's not an afterlife spent with her."

He fell silent for a moment, admiring the ripples that the fish had left behind,

"Do you have a friend like that?" he asked. "Was that your star?"

"Yes," Tiluna said. "But I can't find it anymore. I think it's fallen to a place I cannot follow."

The fisherman nodded, knowing what it was to lose something dear.

"What does your heart tell you?"

"I feel like my heart is broken," she said. "It hurts so very much. I want to start over with a brand-new heart."

"Why would you want to start over?" the fisherman said. "Why waste those years of love? Those tides of tears and broken hearts have made you nothing but human. Your heart is decorated with all the love you have ever known, every person you once held dear, every moment you've ever known peace. No amount of love is ever wasted.

Don't you dare tear it down just to start over."

29

That night Tiluna sat quietly on her raft and looked up to the sky. The night so calm and quiet, but soon something caught her eye.

It flashed just beyond the clouds, in hues of white and silver.

"I know that light," she said to herself.

And of course, she was right. It danced across her tear-stained eyes. A lamp of purest light that shone high, high above.

It was her star.

She had found her lonely star. And her lonely star had found her.

"Hello! Hello!" she yelled with joy, leaping to her feet. "Hello my silver star! Oh how I've missed you!"

Tears were streaming down her face, but this time they were tears of purest joy. For not all tears are shed in sadness.

"You found me! You found me and I found

you! I'm so sorry for leaving you! I love you! I love you and I'll never leave you again!"

She jumped and danced upon her raft, and cried with joyful tears. And in that moment she felt what any lost thing hopes to feel. A feeling that even all the sunsets in the world can never compare to.

"Do you really love me?" replied the star.

Its voice was soft and soothing, but Tiluna could tell that something was wrong.

"Of course I love you," she said. "I've come all this way to find you! I've crossed oceans and islands just to bring you home!"

But the star was not so sure,

"Then why did you leave me?" it said. "Why did you leave me all alone those many nights, spending all your time with your newfound friend. I was so lonely without you."

Tiluna did not know how to reply. She thought her star would be happy to see her. She thought it had loved her.

"They were lost," she said. "They were lost, and they needed a friend."

"I needed a friend too," replied the star. "Without your lighthouse lamp, I never felt so cold in my entire life."

"But where did you go?" Tiluna asked. "I thought you had fallen from the sky! I thought I had lost you forever …"

"I was never really gone," the star replied. "I hid myself because I was jealous. I was jealous of you and your new friend."

Tiluna's heart sank so very heavily upon hearing these words. Her star, her oldest friend in the world, had hid from her on purpose.

"Why?" Tiluna asked. "Why would you hurt me like that? I love you."

"I'm sorry," replied the star. "I was angry, and in my anger I kept to myself. Now I know that was selfish of me. I did not mean to hurt you. Please forgive me."

But Tiluna did not reply, this was a heavy weight to carry.

"I understand if you can't forgive me," sadly said the star, and it began to fade like it did so many nights ago.

"Of course I forgive you," Tiluna finally spoke.

"Of course I forgive you, how on earth could I not. Do you really think that I love you so little, that I have no room left in my heart for forgiveness.

Of course I forgive you, how on earth could I not. Every night I have woken to find you gone, and every night I have cried in your absence.

Of course I forgive you, how on earth could I not! In the cold light of day, I see no stars, and only then do I wish for night to fall. Only then do I wish for just one chance of seeing you again, just for one more night. The million stars that light up the sky are nothing to me! Nothing when I compare them to you.

Of course I forgive you, how on earth could I not. Do you really think that one moment of anger could ruin all those nights we spent with each other.

Of course I forgive you! How on earth could I not."

The star began to brighten, and the night stood perfectly still.

"How lucky I am," it said, "to be loved by someone so kind as you."

30

And that was how I found her. I simply followed the silver star. It shone brightly one night, high above the heavens, far greater than it had ever shined before.

And although I was no astronomer, and no navigator by far, I knew that it was hers. I could somehow feel it. For three nights I sailed on and on, resting only in the day when the star had gone to sleep.

Then, on the fourth night, across the misty moonlit waters, there she was. That lonely little girl, with hair as bright as her guardian star. But they were not lonely anymore.

"My friend!" she yelled across the mist. "Oh how good it is to see you again my friend! I have so much to tell you! I found it! I found my star!"

She told me of her adventures, and of the grown-ups she had met.

But of all she had seen, of everything she had discovered, nothing compared to being reunited with her lonely star. She had finally found what she loved most.

So we set sail to find her lighthouse, to bring it safely home.

31

But, dear reader, life is never that simple. We never found the lighthouse, and the star began to slowly fade night by night. I think it needed the light of the lamp.

And each one of those nights, like her silver star, Tiluna seemed to fade with it. Her hair grew steadily darker and darker, the more her star disappeared into the ever-growing night.

I began to fear that we would never get back, that her star would fade entirely.

We had been at sea for so many days now, that I'd lost count of which day was what. I was missing home so dearly. I would've given anything to get back home.

Anything.

And so it was that on one particular night, I saw a ship far out to sea, and I knew this was our only chance of getting home.

"Tiluna! Look!" I said waking her.

"What is it?"

"I think it's a fishing boat," I said. "I think we're saved!"

But Tiluna didn't seem to share my relief.

"Don't you understand?" I said. "They'll take us to a harbour, we can get back to England!"

"I don't want to go to England," she said. "That's your home. I want to go back to my lighthouse, I miss my lonely star."

"Don't you see," I tried to explain, "we can hire a group of professional explorers in England. We can find your lighthouse and put it on the map where it belongs. Then everyone will know about your lighthouse, and everyone will share the beauty of your star."

But Tiluna didn't reply. I thought she must have just been tired.

Now that I look back, I'm sure she was thinking of what the polar bear had said. How his home was being greedily taken, and I think she feared her lighthouse would be next.

In her mind's eye, I think she saw the merchant selling her island for a profit, and the artist painting pictures of it for money and fame.

She didn't want them anywhere near her island at all. She couldn't let the grown-ups ruin what precious little good there was in this world. She couldn't let her lonely star fall from the sky.

But I, of course, did what all grown-ups inevitably do. I assumed that I knew best, simply because I was older.

"But you promised," she said, almost in a whisper. "You promised we'd bring it home."

I didn't reply.

I was too ashamed to reply.

When she was older, I told myself, she would surely understand.

"They're still a long way off," I said to fill the silence. "They'll spot us by the morning. Just hold tight until dawn, and then we're saved."

Tiluna said nothing. And after a while I began to drift into a deep and hopeful sleep.

But just before I sunk into the land of dreams entirely, I have a faint memory of Tiluna whispering something in my ear.

"When you return to England, I'll just be a memory in your head. But that's okay, for as long as it makes you smile, then that is all I could ever wish for. Tears are where memories go when they don't want to be forgotten. We're all just memories in the end. I hope I'll be a good one."

That night she slipped away when I was sleeping, and quietly sailed off into the night.

And that was the last I ever saw of Tiluna.

That morning I watched the sunrise as if it were to be my last.

32

Upon my return to England, I hired a small fishing boat, and took it out to sea alone.

But no matter how hard I searched, no matter for how many months I sailed the waves over and over, I could never again find that lonely lighthouse lost at sea. Nor could I see the silver star when I looked up to the sky.

Tiluna, and her lighthouse, and her star, had all but gone.

And although I write these words many

years after it happened, I know in my heart that she is still out there. That even now she sails the star-lit sea, ever in search of lost things.

So if you too are lost as lost can be, if you too forget what it's like to be curious, I hope you find that little girl, with hair as silver as her lonely star.

And when you do, do me a favour and be nothing but kind. Tell her that I'm sorry.

Tell her that her lighthouse will never be found by grown-ups. Tell her that I'll make sure of that.

That even if she failed to find her way home, tell her that I've been keeping her star company all this time. That it will never fall from the sky. That it will never again know what it is to be lonely.

I've lived many days since that night, and oh how much I've seen. Days of joy, and some of sadness. Days packed with adventure and some days were nothing happened at all.

I've done a great many things, and lived a great deal more. I've had extraordinary moments that words cannot simply describe. I've lived more in twenty years than some do in a hundred.

But love, curiosity, friendship, these little moments outshine them all by far. They are a thousand silver stars in a night full of darkness.

To think of all us lost grown-ups, sat upon our lonely islands. We are all just little lighthouses lost at sea, ever in search of lost things. And sometimes the sea seems so vast and dark, and those terrible stormy days are full of nothing but tears.

But when we take the time to look up to the sky, to see those thousand little dots of silver, we remember that the best days are yet to come. And the dawn of those days will be worth those nights of a hundred tears.

That sometimes, even on the worst of days, hope is just a thousand little lights in the sky. And just how lucky we are, for we do not need a thousand. One little light is all we need to help us through the dark. One little light is all we need: be it from a lighthouse, or a star.

I hope like me, that if you ever are lost, that if you ever find yourself adrift and far out on a hopeless sea: I hope you find Tiluna.

That once, when you are a grown-up, you have an imaginary friend.

Thank you for reading.

If you enjoyed this book, please be so kind as to leave an honest review.

Although great care has been taken in the making of this book, there are bound to be some errors here and there.

If you spot an error, please be so kind as to email:

WanderingHedgehogPublishing@gmail.com

Printed in Dunstable, United Kingdom